A ROOKIE READER®

THE FISH

By Heather MacLeod

Illustrations by Janice Skivington

ℚP Children's Press®
A Division of Grolier Publishing
New York   London   Hong Kong   Sydney
Danbury, Connecticut

This book is dedicated to Al, Allen, and Mark,
who took me on my first fishing trip
when I was 36 years old.
It is also dedicated to the teachers and all my students
at Hillview Crest School and Cabello School.

Library of Congress Cataloging–in–Publication Data

MacLeod, Heather,
    The fish / by Heather MacLeod.
        p. cm. — (A Rookie reader)
    Summary: After waiting and waiting, a child catches a fish—
only to take pity on it and put it back.
    ISBN 0-516-02029-3
[1. Fishing—Fiction.] I. Title. II. Series.

PZ7.M224985F1   1995   95-12934
[E]—dc20   CIP
                                                         AC

I got my pole,

I got my pail,

I got my can of worms.

I got my bobbers,

hooks, and net

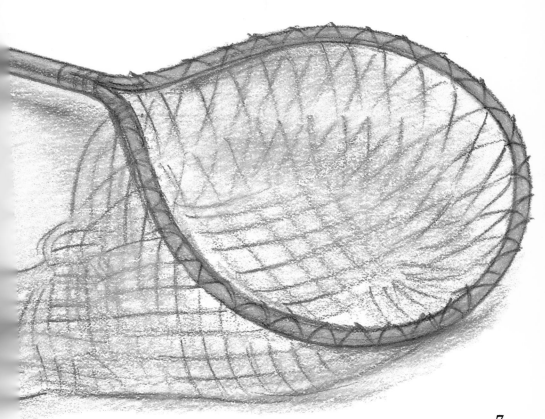

and went out

to catch a fish.

I put the worm on the hook.
It wiggled and it wiggled.

I cast my line into the pond
and waited to catch a fish.

A fly buzzed by, then all was still.
I waited and I waited.

The sun got hot, and still I waited.
I waited and I waited.

A bird flew by, and still I waited.
I waited and I waited.

Then I saw the line wiggle!
It jiggled and it jiggled.

I picked up the pole

and started to reel.

17

I pulled back as hard as I could

and kept on reeling it in.

I felt the fish pull on the line,

so I pulled even harder.

With one last pull, we pulled him out

22

and put him in my net.

He flipped and flopped,
and flopped and flipped,

and wiggled in my hand.

He looked so scared.
He looked so sad.

He couldn't breathe the air up here.

So I looked at him and said, "Goodbye,"

and then I put him back.

I'm glad I caught a fish today,

and I'm glad I put him back.

About the Author

Heather MacLeod is a former school librarian and third grade teacher. She got jealous of how much fun her students had writing stories, so she started writing her own!

About the Artist

Janice Skivington is the daughter, wife, and mother of avid fishermen. She enjoys fishing, as well as drawing, painting, and illustrating books.

The artwork for this book was a family effort, with Janice's husband, four children, and dog Plato all helping in various ways. Plato is an Australian Shepard, a breed of dog without tails.